Kung Fu Kid

'Kung Fu Kid'
An original concept by Katie Dale
© Katie Dale 2021

Illustrated by Antonella Fant

Published by MAVERICK ARTS PUBLISHING LTD

Studio 11, City Business Centre, 6 Brighton Road,

Horsham, West Sussex, RH13 5BB

© Maverick Arts Publishing Limited November 2021

+44 (0)1403 256941

A CIP catalogue record for this book is available at the British Library.

ISBN 978-1-84886-828-1

www.maverickbooks.co.uk

Green

This book is rated as: Green Band (Guided Reading)
It follows the requirements for Phase 5 phonics.
Most words are decodable, and any non-decodable words are familiar,
supported by the context and/or represented in the artwork.

Kung Fu Kid

by Katie Dale

illustrated by
Antonella Fant

Stu was a baby goat.

Everyone called him the Kung Fu Kid!

I like Kung Fu!

I love to jump!

5

But best of all, Stu liked to chop!

Chop! Chop! Chop!

"I can chop everything!" Stu yelled.

Chop! Chop! Chop!

"I can chop the twigs on the path!"
yelled Stu.

Chop! Chop! Chop!

"Thank you, Stu!" tweeted the robin.

"Now I can make a nest!"

"I can chop the long sticks in the park!"
yelled Stu.

Chop! Chop! Chop!

"Thank you, Stu!" barked the dog.

"Now I can play with this stick!"

"I can chop the big logs in the woods!"

yelled Stu.

"Thank you, Stu!" said the beaver.

"Now I can make a dam!"

"I can chop the flat planks
in the garden!" yelled Stu.

"Stu!" yelled Mum.

"What did you do?!"

Oh no! That was not a plank!

That was Mum's bench!

"Did you chop this, Stu?" said Mum.

"Yes," said Stu sadly. "I am so sorry, Mum! I did not mean to. I just like chopping things."

"I can chop the carrots!" said Stu.

Chop! Chop! Chop!

"I can chop the peppers!" said Stu.

Chop! Chop! Chop!

"I can chop everything!" Stu yelled.

Chop! Chop! Chop!

SPLISH! SPLASH! SPLOSH!

It is Kung Fu stew!

"Yum!" said Mum. "Thank you, Stu!"

Quiz

1. Best of all, Stu likes to...
a) kick!
b) roll!
c) chop!

2. What does the robin use the twigs for?
a) To make a nest
b) To play a game
c) To make a dam

3. What does the beaver use the logs for?
a) To play a game
b) To make a dam
c) To make a nest

4. What does Stu chop by accident?
a) Mum's dress
b) Mum's table
c) Mum's bench

5. What food does Stu make?
a) Kung Fu cake
b) Karate cookies
c) Kung Fu stew

Turn over for answers

Book Bands for Guided Reading

The Institute of Education book banding system is a scale of colours that reflects the various levels of reading difficulty. The bands are assigned by taking into account the content, the language style, the layout and phonics. Word, phrase and sentence level work is also taken into consideration.

Maverick Early Readers are a bright, attractive range of books covering the pink to white bands. All of these books have been book banded for guided reading to the industry standard and edited by a leading educational consultant.

To view the whole Maverick Readers scheme, visit our website at www.maverickearlyreaders.com

Or scan the QR code above to view our scheme instantly!

Quiz Answers: 1c, 2a, 3b, 4c, 5c